Holiday Short Stories

Morbier Impossible
A Second Chance
The Magic of Sharing
The Case of the Disappearing Gingerbread City
The Lucia Crown
Down the Memory Aisle

The Lucia Crown

by R.W. Wallace

Copyright © 2021 by R.W. Wallace

Cover by R.W. Wallace

Cover Illustration 387077588 © elena.degano | Depositphotos

Cover Illustration 56021183 © spokart | Depositphotos

All characters and events in this book, other than those clearly in the public domain, are fictitious and any resemblance to real persons, living or dead, is purely coincidental.

All rights reserved. No part of this publication may be reproduced, distributed, or transmitted in any form or by any means, including photocopying, recording, or other electronic or mechanical methods, without the prior written permission of the publisher, except in the case of brief quotations embodied in critical reviews and certain other noncommercial uses permitted by copyright law.

www.rwwallace.com

ISBN ebook: [978-2-493670-04-5]

ISBN paperback: [978-2-493670-03-8]

R.W. WALLACE
Author of the Ghost Detective Series

THE LUCIA CROWN

A Young Adult Holiday Short Story

Chapter One

I DON'T SCARE easily. When all my classmates were freaking in June because the Maths syllabus was so huge, I simply hunkered down, split the thing into more manageable pieces, and set to work. When we go cross-country skiing and we get to that beak-neck downhill toward the end, I don't attempt to brake to be in full control all the way down. I know there's a tiny uphill after that will help me to stop once I reach the bottom, and in the meantime...that descent is such a rush. When I had to read my latest essay in front of the class because the teacher thought it was "profound," I did it with a firm voice and without showing any doubt.

But today we're having a vote about who gets to walk around with a wreath of candles on her head for half an hour —and I'm terrified.

Why? Because I want it too much.

Tomorrow is December 13th, Santa Lucia. Our choir is having a huge concert in the school's gym and all two hundred tickets are already sold out. We're doing our usual repertoire of songs and adding in some mandatory Christmas songs since it's just two weeks before the big day.

And then we're doing Lucia.

It's just the one song, and it's not very long, only three verses. But it's the big, final act. It's the concert's culminating moment and the one that always makes my heart soar.

I love the song, its message of light showing way in the darkness, the way it goes so high the altos have trouble hitting the notes at times, and so low it's the sopranos who suffer. I love the visuals the choir always offers, with everyone in white robes that we borrow from the church for the day, everyone over the age of thirteen with live candles in their hands, and the visual effects the lighting team keeps getting better at every year.

And Santa Lucia. Every year, one girl is elected to represent the saint. She stands a step ahead of the rest of the choir, dressed in the same white robes, but with a wreath of lights in her hair. And she leads the procession that will take us all off stage and across the gym to the exit.

This is my last year with a chance at the role. Actually, it's also the first. Lucia is always one of the high school seniors. We all get just the *one* shot.

The children's choir will also be part of this one song, which is why they've been brought in to vote for the Lucia. I remember how proud I was when I was allowed to vote, to give my voice to who would be the most beautiful representation of the saint. I always had my favorite and sat there staring at the girl in question the whole time we were there, hoping she would notice me.

I see quite a few of the young girls around us doing the same right now. The boys, for the most part, are pretending to be above such silliness and are playing games on their phones. The ones who don't have phones lean in to do commentary on their friends' conquests.

I think a few of the girls are looking at me. Maybe. I did let my hair out of its usual bun on purpose and brushed it to a golden shine before coming.

People tend to like having blonde long-haired Lucias. I don't personally agree that she should be blonde but I'm also not above using it to my advantage, just this once.

I'm pretty sure several of the girls are looking at Nina, though, and not at me. Maybe.

Nina is my best friend and has sung in this choir for one week longer than me. We were both ten and when I first arrived, I was completely lost. Nina, with her one week's worth of experience, showed me around. I basically haven't let her out of my sight since.

Nina *isn't* blonde. She was adopted from South-Korea when she was a baby so even though she sounds and behaves as Norwegian as you can get, physically, she's very different. I find her petite stature, narrow black eyes, and sleek black hair gorgeous, but I don't think she'll get enough votes to be Lucia. I don't think this group is quite there yet.

She's getting *my* vote, of course. If I can't be Lucia, it has to be Nina.

They've set up a new system for voting this year. We're going through some website and everyone can vote using their phones. Then there's a visual representation of our votes on a screen. Seems fun in theory, at least.

"All right, people," Kristin, our director, yells to get everyone to settle down. "We're ready for the vote. When I open the poll, you can type in the name of the girl you want for Lucia. After five minutes, we'll see which three names appear the most often and then have a vote on those three."

"Why only girls?" Perry yells from the back. He's the undisputed king of our high school and should be too cool to be part of a choir but he has the voice of an angel and knows it and has somehow managed to become king of this place too and still stay cool.

I stay as far away from him as I can.

Kristin rolls her eyes. "You can vote for boys, too, if you want. I'm sure you'd look very pretty with a wreath of candles in your hair, Perry."

"Oh, I wasn't thinking about me." And he sends a meaningful glance at Marius.

Marius, who is not very big, not very strong, who makes rumors about him being gay flare every time he does something that doesn't fit with the masculine stereotype. Like singing in a choir.

Talk about double standards.

"People better not follow that jerk's lead," Nina mutters.

Kristin doesn't so much as look at Marius but I see her swallow. "Nobody will be forced to play Lucia. If the winner doesn't want the honors, the runner-up will get the crown. Let's vote."

We all bend over our phones. It's only possible to vote once, so I send in my vote for Nina. As I glance over at my friend, I see her typing in my name. My heart does a little jump in my chest.

On the screen, the votes are appearing in colorful bubbles. Kristin moves them around in clusters, grouping the votes for the same person.

I see several with my own name, quite a few of Nina's—and too many of Marius's.

"All the guys are voting for Marius, aren't they?" I whisper to Nina.

"All right," Kristin says. "All the votes are in." She takes a deep breath. "Before we move to the second round...Marius, do you want us to keep your name in the race?"

I can't see the exact count, but the poor guy wins with quite the margin.

All heads turn to look at Marius. I know he doesn't like the attention but I also can't *not* look at him.

My heart breaks a little when I see his face. He's beet red and clearly would like to be anywhere else but here...but I also think he'd actually like to be Lucia. Girls aren't the only ones who might find the tradition magical.

He shakes his head with jerky movements. Perry and his cronies snicker.

Kristin ignores them. "So Marius is out of the race. This means we'll have a final vote between Aurora, Nina, and Tuva."

Tuva doesn't stand a chance. She only got five votes in the first round and those were from her group of friends, guaranteed. So it's basically between me and my best friend.

I reach out to hold her hand, suddenly needing the reassurance that this won't ruin our friendship.

"Are you making up drama in your head again?" Nina asks.

"Yes."

"Okay." She squeezes my hand and grabs her phone in the other. "I'm voting for you."

I have the worst time unlocking and handling my phone with my left hand but I manage to vote for Nina before the time is up.

As we wait for the vote to finish, my hand is still in Nina's and I'm increasingly aware of that fact. We don't hold hands very often, and if we do, it's for a second or two in passing. This has been going on for a solid minute. And my hand is getting sweaty. My heart is jittery and it's not even for the election.

"Everybody got their votes in?" Kristin gives us half a second to reply before clicking on the "Results" button. "Our next Lucia is…"

My name pops up on the screen.

There's no score so I don't know by how much I won. I'm *glad* I don't know. But I *won*! And Nina *lost*.

Feeling both insanely happy and sorely disappointed at once is very confusing.

Nina hugging me close and congratulating me doesn't help. She smells of lavender from the shampoo I gave her for her birthday last month. I knew that scent would suit her.

I take one deep lungful then extricate myself and smile at all the young girls from the children's' choir.

I'm going to be Lucia.

Chapter Two

THE DAY OF the concert, Friday the thirteenth, backstage in the school gym: complete and utter chaos.

There are nineteen kids, ages ten to thirteen, running around in white robes, with silver tinsel in their hair and each carrying a fake electrical candle, some turning it on and off over and over until Kristin yells at them.

The twelve boys from our choir prance around in their robes, making jokes and blustering in order to cover the fact that they're wearing something that's a little too close to a dress for their comfort. They tell Kristin—just like they did last year and every year before that—that no, they will not wear tinsel in their hair. They will, however, take the candles, I suspect only because it means they're allowed to play with an open flame. Whoever thought *that* was a good idea is an idiot.

The older girls, all twenty-five of us, also have live candles. One girl out of three has a lighter so that we can light up when the time comes. Some have made intricate wreaths of the tinsel they were given, some have weaved it into their braids. Nina is absolutely magnificent with a braid going around her head like a crown and the silver tinsel braided in, making is seem like she has sparkly silver highlights. Her mother is a genius with those braids she always does for her daughter.

My hair is free and cascading down my back. I spent twenty minutes brushing it before coming here. I am going to be the best Santa Lucia *ever*.

"Where's your wreath?" Kristin asks me. Her eyes are a little wild and only the left half of her hair is still inside her ponytail. I don't think it's a fashion statement.

"Uh. I haven't seen it yet. I thought you would bring it to me."

Kristin takes a deep breath and lets it out, slowly. "Every year it's the same thing." She points to the boxes in the back, where all the tinsel and lights have been coming from. "It's in one of those boxes with the rest of the stuff. You're the Lucia; you go find it."

I scurry over to the boxes and start looking through them.

Nina joins me. "What are we looking for?" She's going through a box before I even answer.

"The Lucia wreath."

"Oh! Yeah, might be a good idea to find that one. You know, before the concert starts."

"Not helping."

The concert is scheduled to start in fifteen minutes and the two first boxes yield nothing but tinsel and lights. Next four boxes: same thing.

The wreath isn't in any of the boxes.

"Somebody has already taken it out of the box." I spin around slowly in a circle, really looking at everyone, seeing if anyone has put the Lucia wreath on their own head or if one of the young girls is playing with it.

There are lots of lights but none attached to a wreath made of branches. That thing is the only thing made of wood in the entire procession.

"Perry and his clique aren't here," Nina says.

"Neither is Marius," I say.

Our gazes meet for a second. "We need to find Perry."

A quick look behind the curtain shows the gym filling up with parents but no white figures with a wreath. We work on the assumption that the boys will still be wearing their robes because even if they like causing mayhem, they will not want to actually ruin the concert. They take as much pride in our performance as the rest of us.

We quickly run through the three rooms backstage—nobody there.

Across the lobby and down the hallway to the changing rooms. We pop our heads into the girls' room; empty.

Nina stops in front of the boys' locker room, her hand on the door handle. "We're not allowed in there. We're not boys."

"Nobody's supposed to be changing now. And this is an emergency." I put my hand over hers, feel a little zing shooting up my arm, and pull the door open.

My first thought: I was too quick to accuse Perry.

My second: Wait, no. It *is* Perry.

Marius is standing on one of the benches along the far wall, wearing his white robe, one unlit candle in each hand, tinsel making a criss-crossing pattern across his torso—and the Lucia wreath on his head.

And on our side of the room, with their backs to us, Perry and his clique.

They're holding up their phones, taking pictures of Marius. "Just one more picture, Marius. A couple more seconds and your pretty face will remain unblemished."

Nina rushes through the door, her eyes alight like a beautiful, dark angel. "I'm so happy to learn that you agree he has a pretty face, Perry. What is it about it that you like so much? The cheekbones? The full lips? The blue eyes?"

A small part of my brain is blaring red alert alarms. There are four rather big boys in the room; a group that I *know* like to bully others and don't mind throwing in a fist or two. Then there's Nina and myself; two girls who stopped growing at thirteen. And Marius. The poor boy is frozen in fear on that bench and won't be a help to anybody until someone manages to reboot him.

But where my normal reaction in this situation would be to run away, to get as much distance between me and the danger as possible, I now have an additional element to consider: Nina, standing on tiptoe in front of Perry, squaring off.

I can't let her do this on her own. I will not allow Perry to put any blemishes on *her* skin.

So with absolutely no forethought, I barge into the locker room, finger wagging like I'm an angry grandmother who caught her grandson with his dirty fingers in the cookie dough.

"Perry, what the hell do you think you're doing? Why are you torturing Marius like that? Don't you know the concert starts in, like, five minutes? Seriously, how old are you? Five? You're eighteen, dude! You're supposed to behave like a goddamned adult!"

I'm in his face, right next to Nina, and together we're forming a very angry female wall that reaches Perry's chin, approximately.

I start to run out of steam but Perry is wide-eyed and clearly in shock that someone is standing up to him, a situation I need to take full advantage of.

I swerve to the right to go up to Marius and pull him down from the bench. "Come on, Marius. We're out of here. Let's go get ready for the concert." As we pass the group of bullies, I once again point my finger at Perry. "Kristin will hear of this."

Shouldn't have said that. Heat rises in Perry's cheeks and his chest visibly inflates as he prepares his counter-attack.

Time to retreat. I grab Nina with my free hand and pull all three of us out the locker room door and down the hall toward the gym.

We run into Kristin backstage. Her ponytail has disappeared completely and a sheen of sweat is visible both on her forehead and on her neck. "Where were you guys? We're about to start. Marius! Why are you wearing the wreath?"

I yank the wreath off Marius's head and put in on mine. "Don't worry, Kristin. We're ready." I pull the tinsels off Marius's body, probably hurting him in the process but not caring.

As we run for the stage, I hear Perry and his goons exiting the locker room and Kristin swearing under her breath when she puts two and two together.

Chapter Three

I'M NOT SUPPOSED to actually wear the crown until the Lucia song at the end, so I pull it off as we take our places on the soprano side of the choir. The plan was for me to put the wreath off to the side behind the curtain but the murderous look on Perry's face when he takes up his spot in the back makes me change my mind. I keep it in my hand and hold my hands behind my back so the audience won't see it.

The concert is great. Not a single false start or off-tune note in sight and Kristin visibly relaxes as we plow through our repertoire and the audience obviously loves everything.

Then it's time for the Santa Lucia song.

The lights are dimmed so we can only see each other's white robes and the emergency exit lights. The audience, who knows the drill, keeps quiet.

The children's' choir, who have somehow managed to stay calm in the back rooms during the entire concert, march out and take up their places in front of us. They each have their fake candles lit, giving them a very soft glow just strong enough to light up their little faces.

And I step up to the very front, putting the crown on my head but leaving it unlit.

Kristin counts down from three, and the children start singing.

"Svart senker natten seg..."

While they sing of the black night, the room stays dark. I reach up to the wreath, finding the switch that will turn on the lights. God, I wish I'd had the time to test it before coming on stage.

As the children start the line where Lucia appears, I flip the switch.

The wreath lights up.

We do this every year and the audience is pretty much the same every year, since it's mostly our parents, friends, and relatives. And yet, every year, there's a general intake of breath when the Lucia appears.

This year is no exception.

For the second verse, the girls in our choir join in. They quickly light their candles and the light surges in synch with the volume of the song.

I also light my candle but I don't sing. I'm just to stand there and look serene as I light the way through the darkness.

I see several hands on hearts and glittering eyes in the audience, including my parents out on the right wing.

For the third and final verse, the boys join in. More lights, more volume. More depth, especially with Perry's beautiful tenor carrying us all to new heights.

This is what I always associate with singing in a choir. This magical moment, with the beautiful song starting out low in the belly and finishing off way up in the clouds. The feeling of being part of a group, being carried by a team.

And this year I get to be the central figure, like I always dreamed of.

The last notes taper off and the gym is left in silence. One newbie parent starts applauding but is quickly silenced by his neighbors. Most of them know the drill.

It's time for the procession.

The youngest children swarm forward and form two lines, one going past on each side of me. They walk carefully down the stairs leading down from the stage and start down the aisle separating the audience in two.

I'm next, then the rest of the choir. Nina comes in right behind me, on the right. On the left...Perry.

How did he manage to make his way up front from his spot at the very back?

No matter. I have a job to do.

I walk carefully down the short flight of stairs, taking care not to move my head too much for fear the crown will fall off—that happened to one girl three years ago and I will *not* make the same mistake—and proceed down the aisle after the children.

When they reach the last row of the audience, they scatter in all directions. It's officially the end of the procession. They have very strict instructions to stay quiet until everybody has arrived but they're allowed to move.

As I reach the end, I let out a breath I must have been holding in since I left the stage. I did it. I was Lucia and it was *awesome.*

The next thirty seconds feel like they last thirty minutes. I'm not even sure I understand what happens.

There's the smell of something burning.

Nina yelling, "What the hell—!"

One of the girls behind me exclaiming, "Oh my god!" in that tone that's supposed to be shocked but is actually closer to gleefully thrilled.

And Perry's, "Oops." Plus a chuckle.

Next thing I know, I'm lying on the floor with Nina straddling my waist. The crown goes flying and I hear a crunching sound that must be from at least one of the candles breaking.

Nina is hitting me.

Wait, no.

She's hitting something right next to my head.

My hair.

"There," Nina says, still banging her flat palm on my hair spread out on the floor. "It's out. I think. You!" She pulls on the coattails of a woman walking past. "Give me your water!" She grabs the woman's half-empty water bottle and empties it on my hair. And my face.

I blink, several times, trying to get the water out of my eyes. Only now do I notice that Nina has my arms pinned to my side and I cannot move.

"I'm so sorry," Nina babbles. She runs her hand over my face, wiping away the water. Her eyes widen. "Oh shit, your mascara."

As she bends down to see better and draws one finger gently under my left eye, I'm surrounded by her lavender scent, with just a touch of singed hair. I should care about the hair part, I really should.

But all I can think about is how close she is. How intently she's staring at my face as she cleans it up. How soft her lips look.

"Perry!" Kristin's shout makes me jerk so hard I manage to free one hand and Nina almost pokes my eye out.

"That is the *last* straw! You will not show your face in this choir ever again, you hear me? Your parents are going to hear about this! Oh, wait. Are they here? Are Perry's parents here tonight? Where? I want them."

I don't actually see any of the drama going on around me. I only see Nina's widening eyes and her hand shaking so badly I'm afraid she might have another stab at my eye—literally.

I grab her shaking hand with my free one and pull them out of my line of sight. "Nina?" I say softly. "We need to get up before someone steps on us."

We are, after all, lying flat on the floor in the middle of a crowd of more than two hundred people. Just to be on the safe side, we're in the direct path of anyone who wants to reach the sweets being set out on a table in the back.

Nina scrambles off me, kneeing me in the thigh, and I jump up after her. She's about to run off, but I hold her back. I haven't let go of her hand.

"Wait," I say. "How bad is my hair?"

At the moment, I don't really care that much, but I know that's going to change once the adrenaline wears off. Still, it can't be that bad. I see hair everywhere and can already tell it's going to take me hours to get all the knots out tonight.

Getting Nina to focus on my problems was the right thing to do. Her eyes come back into focus as she gingerly pulls the hair from my back over my right shoulder. "He set fire to the part in the middle of your back. But it didn't get very far up before we stopped it." She holds up a strand of hair with blackened and curled ends. The burnt smell from earlier returns.

Sighing, I grab the hair. Pull out some that hasn't been burned.

I'm missing about ten centimeters.

Kind of a lot but then I had a lot to begin with.

"Guess I'll be getting a haircut," I say. I try to sound casual but my voice breaks a little on the last word. Dammit.

Nina gently pulls the singed hair out of my hands and moves it back out of sight. Then she finger-brushes the rest, pushing it out of my face and generally doing her best to make me presentable.

Marius comes up to us, the broken wreath in one hand. "You dropped this," he says.

"Right." I look at the poor thing. Two of the six candles are broken and the wreath itself seems to be somewhat bent out of shape. "I don't..." I recognize the look in his eyes suddenly. It's the way I looked at that thing every single year up until now. "Maybe you should hold on to it until Kristin needs it again?"

"I don't..."

"Maybe you could fix the candles," Nina says. "Someone needs to get on that."

Marius knows what we're doing but I'm happy see him come to the conclusion that he doesn't care. Perry hasn't broken him yet. Nodding, he walks off toward the stage, cradling the wreath against his chest.

"How about some lussekatter?" Nina asks, her beautiful dark eyes staring straight into mine.

There are two great things about Santa Lucia. One is the song with the lights and the crown and the tassels. The other is the lussekatter. The special buns made with dried raisins and saffron. The saffron makes them yellow—apparently a trick to scare away the devil. Also works for attracting hungry girls.

Grabbing Nina's hand again, I pull her toward the table. "Great idea," I say. I grab four buns, ignoring the glare of the mother standing behind the table, and cradle them against my chest. "How about we take them to go? My house is empty right now."

My eyes widen at the same time as Nina's. Seems like none of us expected me to issue that challenge.

Nina takes it, though. "Sounds great." Then she squeezes my hand.

About the Author

R.W. Wallace writes in most genres, though she tends to end up in mystery more often than not. Dead bodies keep popping up all over the place whenever she sits down in front of her keyboard.

The stories mostly take place in Norway or France; the country she was born in and the one that has been her home for two decades. Don't ask her why she writes in English—she won't have a sensible answer for you.

Her Ghost Detective short story series appears in *Pulphouse Magazine*, starting in issue #9.

You can find all her books, long and short, all genres, on rwwallace.com.

Also by R.W. Wallace

Mystery

Ghost Detective Novels

Beyond the Grave

Unveiling the Past

Beneath the Surface

Ghost Detective Shorts

Just Desserts

Lost Friends

Family Bonds

Common Ground

Till Death

Family History

Heritage

Eternal Bond

New Beginnings

Severed Ties

Ghost Detective Collections

Unfinished Business, Volume 1

Mystery Collections

Deep Dark Secrets

A Thief in the Night

Time Travel (short stories)

Moneyline Secrets

Family Secrets

Romance

French Office Romance Series

Flirting in Plain Sight

Hiding in Plain Sight

Loving in Plain Sight

Short Stories

Down the Memory Aisle

Holiday Short Stories

Morbier Impossible

A Second Chance

The Magic of Sharing

The Case of the Disappearing Gingerbread City

The Lucia Crown

Down the Memory Aisle

Young Adult Collections

Tales From the Trenches

Science Fiction (short stories)

The Vanguard

rwwallace.com/allbooks

www.ingramcontent.com/pod-product-compliance
Lightning Source LLC
LaVergne TN
LVHW040204080526
838202LV00042B/3316